The Mystery
The Foggy Day

Collins

An imprint of HarperCollins*Publishers*

It was a very foggy day in Toyland...

BRRING! BRRING!
Noddy jumped out
of bed and switched off
his alarm clock. Then
he remembered why he
had to get up. It was
Miss Pink Cat's birthday.

At the beginning of the week, Mr Sparks had asked Noddy to collect presents from everyone in Toy Town.

Noddy was to deliver the presents to Miss Pink Cat's house very early on the day of her birthday. She would get a lovely surprise when she woke up.

What a lot of presents there were!

"I wish it were *my* birthday," sighed Noddy as
he put all the presents in a large sack and opened
his front door.

Imagine Noddy's surprise when he looked outside.
He couldn't see his red and yellow car *or*
Master Tubby Bear's house next door! Toy Town
was covered in thick fog.

"My little car must be here
somewhere!" Noddy took three steps to
the side and bumped into something.

"There you are, little car, I've found you!" said
Noddy. He climbed in, switched on the lights and
started to drive forwards slowly.

BUMP! He drove straight into a tree.

"I can't see where I'm driving!" wailed Noddy. "It's no good, I'll have to walk."

He picked up the sack of parcels and started to walk very slowly and carefully towards Miss Pink Cat's house. After a little while, he realised he was totally lost.

"Oh, dear!" he said. "These presents are going to arrive very late and Mr Sparks will be cross."

Suddenly, through the fog, he heard a sound. It was Big-Ears, singing a happy song.

"Thank goodness!" said Noddy. "I must be at
Big-Ears' house. If I follow this path for ten minutes
and then turn left, I will arrive at Miss Pink Cat's
house on time!"

Ten minutes later, he found himself outside
somebody's front door.

"This must be Miss Pink Cat's house," said
Noddy, and he posted the presents through the door.

As he was leaving he heard the sound of someone giggling nearby. It sounded just like Master Tubby Bear. But it couldn't be! He would be at home having breakfast.

Feeling puzzled, Noddy set out to try to find his way home, but he got lost again! This fog certainly made everything very tricky.

He walked along for ten minutes more and this time, through the fog, he heard Tessie Bear humming a little tune as she baked her cakes.

The smell of Tessie's cakes led Noddy all the way to her door.

"Hello, Noddy," said Tessie. "I have just taken Miss Pink Cat's birthday cake out of the oven. Would you like some breakfast?"

"Yes, please," replied Noddy.

After breakfast, as Noddy walked home, the fog lifted and the sun began to shine. "What a lovely sunny day," said Noddy to himself as he arrived at his house.

"Oh, no, it isn't!" said a voice. Noddy looked around and saw a very cross-looking Mr Plod coming towards him.

"Mr Sparks has reported you for running away with all Miss Pink Cat's birthday presents," said Mr Plod.

But as Mr Plod marched towards Noddy, he tripped over his own bootlace. CRASH! He fell over in a heap.

Noddy jumped into his car and drove off.

"I'm sorry, Mr Plod," he called, "but I have to find the missing presents."

He drove straight to Big-Ears' house and told him the whole story.

"What a mystery," said Big-Ears.

"We must find the presents," said Noddy, "to prove that I'm not the thief!"

The two friends searched all over Toy Town.
But nobody had seen the birthday presents.

"We need to start at the beginning," said Big-Ears. "Let's think about everything you did this morning."

They drove back to Noddy's house and, on the way, Noddy started his story all over again.

"I heard you singing," said Noddy, "so I knew I must be at your house and..."

"But I wasn't at home this morning!" said Big-Ears.

"I had to collect a parcel from the early morning train. I was in Market Crescent when I sang that song."

"So I wasn't at your house at all!" said Noddy. "Then I must have taken the presents to the wrong house!"

"But which one?" asked Big-Ears.
    Noddy thought hard.

Suddenly he remembered something.
"I heard Master Tubby Bear giggle!" he said.

"So the presents are at the Tubby Bears' house?" asked Big-Ears.

Noddy laughed. "No," he said. "They're here!"

He opened his front door and there, just inside the door were Miss Pink Cat's presents!

Noddy had delivered them to his own house by mistake!

Noddy and Big-Ears collected Tessie Bear and drove to Miss Pink Cat's house.

"Happy Birthday, Miss Pink Cat!" said Noddy as they arrived. He told everyone what had happened.

"What a foggy muddle!" said Mr Sparks. "Here is your coin, Noddy. You've earned it!"

FROM SLY & GOBBO

"He certainly has!" said Big-Ears. "He solved the mystery of the missing presents just in time!"

Everyone cheered, including Miss Pink Cat, who had a very happy birthday after all.

FROM MR SPARKS

Here are some more books for you to enjoy:

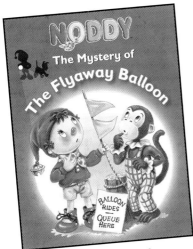

The Mystery of
The Flyaway Balloon
ISBN 0-00712359-0

The Mystery of
The Stolen Bicycles
ISBN 0-00712361-2

The Mystery of
The Missing Friends
ISBN 0-00712358-2

For further information please contact www.NODDY.com

This edition first published in Great Britain by HarperCollins Publishers Ltd in 2002

1 3 5 7 9 10 8 6 4 2

Copyright © 2002 Enid Blyton Ltd. Enid Blyton's signature mark and the words "NODDY" and "TOYLAND" are Registered Trade Marks of Enid Blyton Ltd.
For further information on Enid Blyton please contact www.blyton.com

ISBN: 0 00712360 4

Reproduction by Graphic Studio S.r.l. Verona
Printed in China by Jade Productions